Moon Shine

Flairs and Glairs

Publication House

"MoonShine"

ISBN No: " 978-93-90799-72-5"
1st Edition
Language – English and Hindi

Flairs and Glairs
Publication House
Regd. Under MSME Act.

Disclaimer

This is a work of fiction and solely represent the thoughts of the corresponding authors of the articles. Our editors have tried their best to edit the content of all the authors and check the plagiarism.
All the write-ups in this book are unique and are only published in this book.
In case any plagiarism or error is found, only the author is responsible alone, and not the publisher or the Compilers.

Cover Designing and Book Formatting
Shubham Shah and Ishani Agarwal

Acknowledgement

Dear God, thank you for your blessings, Also thanks to my family they did everything for me. The compilation of this anthology would have not been possible with the support of Co-authors.

A very big thanks to all the Co-authors and the entire team who have been working with us and gave their precious time to us.

Special thanks to Aditya Srivastava and Deepanshi Raikwar for guiding me and supporting me althrough..

Thanks to Deepanshi Raikwar for helping me get some co-authors for this anthology Thank you all of you for being there.

Sona Agarwal & Rhagavi

Co-Author

Shubham Shah (Founder Flairs and Glairs)
Ishani Agarwal (Co-Founder Flairs and Glairs)

1. Sona Agarwal (Compiler)
2. Rhagavi (Co-Compiler)
3. Deepanshi Raikwar (Project Head)
4. Nilanjana Sarkar
5. Adlin Sweety
6. Akshaya
7. M.Aysha Sahanaz
8. D.V.Pimputkar
9. A.Dhanya Lakshmi
10. A.Faheema Banu
11. J.Gayathri
12. Gurleen Kaur
13. M.Ilakiya
14. Jacob Rosario
15. M.Jayasankari
16. Kathijathul Kubra
17. Kowsalya Thangadurai
18. S. Malini
19. T.Monisha
20. Pragya Verma
21. Prathamesh Pravin Naik
22. Praveena Ramesh
23. Rashmi Baweja
24. V. Sai Gayathri
25. S.Saraswetha
26. S. Shalini
27. P.Sharmila
28. Sofiya Mehake

29. Swayamdeepta Das
30. Vaishali Lakshmanan
31. Yamini Sona Vaishnavi
32. S.Yasmin
33. Zeel Milishia
34. Ankita Pande
35. M.V.Anandhi
36. Sai Charu
37. P.Deebika
38. Sanjoli Mittal
39. Divyank Raj
40. Krishna Motwani
41. Gowri
42. Sehrish Fuzel
43. Sachin Banoudhiya
44. Diksha Motwani
45. Jata
46. Vibhor Bijoy
47. Khushi Gupta
48. Elia Naqvi
49. Anindita Bhattacharya
50. Pratham Mittal
51. Bickey Mandal
52. Saniya Mahek
53. Priya Das
54. Nikhil Jain
55. Leena Devi Nedunchezhiyan

Shubham Shah

(Founder- Flairs and Glairs)

Shubham Shah, an entrepreneur at "Flairs & Glairs" a brand with dynamics in events organizing and cultural educational pan INDIA, is a 26yrs old guy who recently has entered the digital platform of imprinting emotions. He has initiated with

his own open mic platform to help budding poets and aspiring writers under his brand named as "Teekhe Zasbaaat"
He is a commerce graduate from the Bhagalpur City of Bihar. He states Writing has impersonated him since childhood and he has now been writing for over a decade!
Cooking, on the other hand, is his passion! He also mentions, trying out new things just tickles him!
When asked sir, Why SPICY EMOTIONS?
He smiled and added, "agar jasbaat teekhe na ho toh wo jasbaat kahan" Spices are all that blends! So do his words!
As a chef, he presents to you his dish! Hot and freshly served! Taste it! Feel it! Enjoy it! You can also find his writing in the Book "Teekhe Zasbaaat" and 50+ Co-authored anthologies. With his passion to explore opportunities across Platforms, he is working with keen devotion and We wish him all the very best for his future ventures.
He is Featured in the **International Magazine De-Mode** for his upcoming solo novel.
He is **Approved by Ne8x for its Lit Fest,** and is a **Golden Star Awards 2020 Winner.**
He is an **India Book of Records Holder** for his Anthology **Satrang,** and has the **Grandmaster** title by **Asia Book of Records**, for the same.
He has also been featured in **Prabhat Khabar**, **Dainik Jagran** and other renowned Newspaper for his achievements.
He has also been awarded with **India Star Republic Award 2021.**
He has been a proud co-author to
India Book of Records (Title- Black)
World Book of Records (Title -15 Wonders of Poetries)
India Book of Records (Title - Aaina)
Vajra World Records Holder (Title - Gustakhi Maaf Hai)

High Range of Records Holder (Title - Gustakhi Maaf Hai)

Share your reviews on his

INSTAGRAM
@spicy_emotions
@shubham4shah

Or via email on
shubham2shah@gmail.com

To stay tuned to his work and opportunities follow his business Handles

INSTAGRAM FACEBOOK YOUTUBE

@flairsandglairs
@teekhezasbaaat

WEBSITE:
https://flairsandglairs.in/
https://flairsandglairs.com/

Ishani Agarwal

(Co-Founder- Flairs and Glairs)

Ishani Agarwal hails from the City of Joy, Kolkata.
She is the co-founder of her Community "Teekhe Zasbaaat" and Flairs and Glairs Publication.
Been a Compiler for 45+ Anthologies, she is in the process for more. Co-authored in 150+ Anthologies. She is a India Book of Records Holder, a Vajra World Records Holder, a High Range of Records Holder and a Bravo Record holder.

Approved by Ne8x for its Lit Fest 2020, and Literary Icon 2020. Also a Golden Star Awards Winner 2020.
She has also been awarded with India Star Republic Award 2021.
She has been featured by the National Magazine "Taree Zameen Par" with the title 'unstoppable'.
Also featured in the International Magazine DeMode for her upcoming solo novel, she is proud to write on social issues, and is happy with the love she is receiving.
Connect with her on Instagram: @Ishani_agarwal_quotes / @compilations_so_far

SONA AGARWAL
(COMPILER)

The Young Emerging Author SONA AGARWAL is just 21 who is pursuing her graduation in the field of commerce, residing in Villupuram town within TamilNadu. She loves to enjoy the every moment of the life instead of doing or travelling in one path. She doesn't needed any fame for her works instead of which she needed to enjoy the journey in every possible way till her heart fills up. She writes not to fill the pages with words but with feelings from her heart. The feelings play a major role for every writer. The heart seeks the feelings not the words after all.*Instagram handle: ahana__writes*

MUMMA'S QUEEN DADDA'S ARMY

Someday you gonna arrive
Near your Momma and Dadda,
With ten little buttery fingers,
Ten little toes to walk along with us,
The dream will all of yours,
And May I become the wings for that?
Your dadda will be so stupid,
While watching us flying together,
He may shout and he may jealous,
But what can I do when,
I gave birth to my little queen,
Momma will be yours,
Queen you are for the world,
May the dream of your arrival,
Blessed with the God,
You are my whole universe,
Just to be my love,
You dream the whole world,
With your tiny pretty eyes,
Will be your lashes,
To safeguard you everytime

RHAGAVI
(CO-COMPILER)

Rhagavi hails from Tamilnadu; she is a girl with million dreams.She discovered her passion in literature few years ago and started scribbling her thoughts out.She hopes to write more and more to support people virtually, she believes her words could make someone smile somewhere and she is trying hard to make everyone believe in the universe.She can be contacted at rhagvisha73@gmail.com.Her IG handle is @secretbehindwords

STARS AND THE DREAMS

When you talk about dreams you can compare many things with it but what hits my mind first are stars, there are infinite stars, we can't count them as same as the dreams,we will have spark for everything but we fail to shine in some but what we have is enough to lighten our whole universe.That's the magic of stars and magic of dreams.They give you a reason not to give up no matter what. Even in childhood days we would have been mad on stars we would have been kept on counting but ended in vain. But still the next day we used to do the same, when there are only few stars we will feel happy because we can count them and would have felt like receiving an award. That night we will have inner peace and a big wide smile before sleep.

You will face many hardships while working for your dream you may fall, you may feel like giving up, you may be tired of everything but still heart wants what it wants, the next day you'll have the same strength that you had on your first day of stepping towards your dream and trust me success is no longer far away your gonna reach it soon just like that twinkling stars your dreams are gonna make you shine. And that day all your hard works will be paid off. You will be proud about yourself for making it possible that's the day you have proved god your existence. Never give up on your dreams, stick on to it, achieve it and overcome all the pain by enjoying the success.

DEEPANSHI

A technophile girl with beautiful dreams and high hopes in life. With both optimistic and pessimistic ideology. Deepanshi Raikwar, hailing from City Of Lakes - Bhopal. She loves to write about love and life and mostly about the broken hearts of young minds. She is a young amazing writer; she is a lively, kind-hearted girl with a dramatic and enthusiastic personality. She is a National Paddler and a good Debater too. She is an Ethical hacker, certified by CCNA. To see more of her work you can follow her on @sakhii__writes

सपना

सपना देखा मैंने एक प्यारा-सा,
पता है क्या देखा ..?
पेडों पर लगी चॉकलेट,
तोड़ो और खाओ।
रोकनेवाला कोई नहीं,
मौज मनाओ।
चाँद-तारे आये नीचे,
मछली उड़े आकाश में।
बच्चे बन गए टीचर,
और टीचर पड़े क्लास में।
खेल-खेल में हुई पढ़ाई,
परीक्षा हुई आसानी से।
हस्ते-गाते रहे कोई झूमे,
दुख-दर्दगया आकाश में।
आँख खुली तो था वो सपना,
कुछ न रहा मेरा अपना।।

NILANJANA SARKAR

This is Nilanjana Sarkar. She hails from West Bengal, Alipurduar and currently she's studying in class 12 and working as a head of the Publication in WYIMUN on based on the three committee WHO, UNHRC and UNDP. She's also working as an Entrepreneur with team Elite which deals with E-commerce, direct selling and social media platforms, she's is very hardworking and passionate girl. She is an impulsive writer who oozes out her emotions and feelings and thoughts via writing. *Instagram handle: nataliaboris69*

Tell me
He asked
About our house
About our children
And our gardens
About the life we will
One day have tell me
But she never did
Because it wasn't real
And it wasn't until she was gone
That she understood
That he never needed the house
She only needed the dream

ADLIN SWEETY

She is Adlin Sweety who is just 20 and residing in Villupuram, Tamilnadu. She has completed her training in the field of Teaching. She likes to travel the whole place and engaged herself with paintings, shopping and spending the precious time with her friends

*Instagram handle: _messy_*kid

ACHIEVE

Falling Down is an Accident.
Staying Down is a Choice.

Focus on Your Potential Instead of Your Limitations.

Wait for One but, Don't wait
For Someone to be the ONE.

PATIENCE

Every Problem is Like a RED Signal,
If You wait Sometime,It Will Turn Into GREEN.

Never let the things You want make You forget the things
You have .

A Quiet Mind is able to Hear Intuition Over Fear.

A Man Who is MASTER of PATIENCE is MASTER of
EVERYTHING.

AKSHAYA

She born and brought up in Cuddalore Tamil Nadu. She is 19. She is the odd one who stays constant. Her works are such pure from her heart. She crossed many struggle in her live. She motivate and advice everyone to grow up.
Instagram: akshyav571

BEAUTIFUL DAY

A beautiful sunrise and a new day,
Good morning for today
Wish you have a lovely morning,
Wish you have a lovely day
Everything is special this day,
Everything is new,
You feel the dew,
You feel the air,
Morning is to cheer,
Have a lovely morning

AYSHA SAHANAZ

She is M. Aysha Sahanaz. She is studying 2nd BBA. She is 19 years old. She has positive minds. Her hobby is doing crafts.

Instagram handle: sahanazaysha

BEAUTY OF DREAMS

- Your dream will happen one day, when you'll work for it.
- Dream dream dream...... until you achieve it!
- Life will be more beautiful, when you have dreams.
- To achieve the goals in life, dream it and achieve it.
- If you believe in yourself, your dream will come true!

DEVRAJ PIMPUTKAR

Wanderlust and explorer, Civil Engineer from Pune
Instagram handle: rg_0018

PIECE OF DREAMS

Life was a broken winged bird
Whining in the busy roadside
A quiet pain of shattered dreams
Wimping near the cold tide a hand of hope settles on the shoulder
"Some needs to be forgotten some are meant to broke
If you work for a reason why it happened
Let the tears wipe away and bring a wide smile" she said
Like a mountain stopping the tides cross land I stand
Let me live the life I dreamt
Let the hurdles cross-by because
After the cold winter, it's time to bloom.

DHANYA LAKSHMI

She is doing 4th BNYS, poetry is her passion
Instagram handle: Dhanyalakshmi24

POSITIVE VIBES

In an every negative situation, there will be a positive one.
Yeah, I'm damn sure that, positive vibes

When I tired during sick, I take rest.
When I abused (at social media), I aware.

When I cried, I become stronger
When my dad has struggling financially low, I won't take loan
When my bestie got breakup, I won't fall for fake one
When my neighbourhood got COVID_19 +ve, I would be serious and take precaution
And finally I woke up because it's my entire dream
Conclusion is every negativity has positivity

FAHEEMA BANU

She is Faheema. She loves writing and reading. She believes god deeply. She is doing her UG in psychology. She is from Trichy. She has written few blogs and poems in the pen name of purple. She always wanted to express her thoughts, words and to spread love and positivity.
Instagram handle: purple_.scribbles

DREAM

If you dream, believe,
Your life will be a cream.
If you think deep,
Ideas crawl and creep,
Your deeds will peek,
It makes you freak,
For the success you seek.
Being happy is a dream,
Being rich is a dream.
The seed of every invention,
Is a dream.
It will spread green,
If you plan it clean.
If you feel boredom,
Dream for the freedom.
If you feel upset,
Dream for the set-up.
Dream like nothing can stop you,
It makes everyone to spot you.
Dream, dream, dream...
Like the universe never dreamt before!

GAYATHRI

She is Gayathri from Villupuram, Tamilnadu. She loves literature. Currently she is pursuing her Bachelor's degree in literature. She is fond of writing poems and conveys it in simple and easy way to the reader.
Instagram handle: gayathri0004

THE DREAM

Dream Yourself........
Have dream to achieve goals in life
Having dreams cherish you to achieve target
The desires comes in your life, when
You hold dreams about it.
Dreams should be complicated
They should force you to work hardly.
Have a dream, set it as your goal
Make a plan and brings it to action.
Having confidence brings victory in life
The future depends upon you
Until you believe in beauty of your dream.

GURLEEN KAUR

Her Name is Gurleen Kaur. She is born and brought up in Delhi. She is pursuing her graduation in tourism studies and French language. Her hobbies are writing, dancing and painting. She likes to express herself through words. She aspires to become a famous writer.
Instagram handle: ginnihayer_30

MEET ME IN MY DREAMS

Come to meet me in my dreams,
When I am smiling in my sleep,
Hug me tight and kiss me deep.
There will be love talks,
With those nights walks.
Holding my face with your hands,
Plant a kiss me on my forehead.
I will place my head in your lap,
To cover the gap.
Pull my cheeks slowly,
That beautiful moment of love,
Will pass happily.
Just come once in my dreams,
We will make lots of beautiful memories.

ILAKIYA

She is M.Ilakiya D/o,R.MUTHUKUMARAN from DEPARTMENT OF BUSINESS ADMINISTRATION in the institute of THEIVANAI AMMAL COLLEGE FOR WOMENS, VILLUPURAM. She used to express her thoughts in the way of writing poem and quotes. So she grabbed this opportunity and she participated in this writing.

I USED TO DREAM

I used to dream
By seeing the cloud
Cloud may fade
But, one day my dream will make me over grade.

I used to dream
By seeing the road
Road may end
But, one day my dream will make me Legend.

I used to dream
By seeing the light
Light may turn off
But, one day my dream will make me Hats off.

JACOB ROSARIO

He is Jacob Rosario of 17. He is currently pursuing his 12th STD. He is from Tindivanam. His ambition is to become "President of India". He is a Writer in a page of Instagram @quotes_fromhertmaker. His dream is to Rule the Country. This is his debut book as a co-author.
Instagram handle: jack_rio18

DREAM OF REAL BOY

A boy of 18 was living in a small town.He was born in a Middle class family but he has a dream to Rule the Country.

"He was born to Rule,
Not to be Slave for anyone"

When he was studying in school, he had a dream to rule the school and was so confident in his dream. While he was studying at 5th grade he had participated in primary School People Leader Election but his willingness to win was lost. He cannot even tie his head outside. He had that pain for two years and was ashamed of himself. But he didn't lose his hope. When he was studying 7th he had participated in Junior ASPL and he won. From there his dream started to become true. At last he became SCHOOL PEOPLE LEADER.

Read what you like,
Play what you can,
Talk what you know,
But
Dream what you are.

His dream never stopped.He had a love, and had dreamt to marry within 21years and because of which he wanted to become IAS in his 21.After becoming IAS though he had a sophisticated Life of IAS officer his desire yet now is not accomplished.

"Dreams has no Break
But
Dreamers had break to Dream"

He was stable in his Ambition and Dream. He wants to become President of India.

"Your attitude tells you how you are going to be,
But
Your dream tells you what you are going to be"

Fill the Life with your Dreams. Live your life with Happiness.

JAYASANKARI

She is JayasankariMurugan ... She is 19 residing in Villupuram, Tamil Nadu. She is passionate about Photography. She gets on well with all kinds of people. Love the people who love her! Born to achieve something!!!..... Twitter @Jayasankari9

DEAR SOCIETY!!!!

I'm Skinny!!!!....
And I don't starve myself
I'm HEALTHY and HAPPY
Don't tell me to eat more!!
I probably eat more than you think!!
Don't tell me to gain weight.
Don't try to push your ideals on me in anyways,
I'm PERFECT the way I am!!!
If you can feel good about yourself being big,
Then I can feel good about myself for being small!!!!!!!
As the way you are beautiful
As the same way I'm too BEAUTIFULL!

KATHIJATHUL KUBRA

She born and bought up in Villupuram, Tamilnadu. She is 19.She is the odd one who stays constant. Her words are such pure from her heart. She crossed many struggles in her lives but she won't give up on her achievements so that made her strong .She is much sensitive .Though she is broken inside.
Twitter: kathijathulkubra

FAR YOU ARE BUT NEAR TO MY SOUL

You are in my conscious state
When though you made me cry, laugh, implore,
Those days are indelible.
You are in my first sense,
Which always blink first
Can't even imagine those days,
Which that much mixed in our pristine soul
My soul shakes when you leave for a second
Your words are such allegiant
When it compared to be others
You are my boon. You are gift of god
Even though I reach to my deadline
My last words and thought will be yours…

KOWSALYA THANGADURAI

KowsalyaThangadurai, loves literature. Currently she is pursuing her Bachelor's degree in Literature (B.A). She is very fond of writing poems, quotes, etc....Apart from writing she is interested in sports.

HIS PRESENCE IN MY DREAM

At a dark night,
Surrounded by candle light.
He was waiting for me!
While I entered,
His sight was only on me!
He wanted me to look upon his face, and
I slowly raised mine towards him!
His eyes!!
Where I saw the true love!
Then, heard some unwelcomed voice
I opened my eyes
Yes, he is not here
Forever waiting for you my dream boy!!!!!

MALINI

She is Malini from Villupuram. She is doing her graduation in bachelor of commerce her hobby is drawing. She has love on her brother which makes her to shower her words in the poem
Instagram handle: Artshine26

DREAM, HOW MY BROTHER IS?

Have a little brother,
Who is very cute?
Sometimes he hurts,
Who is very naughty!

Shouts at me,
Beat me a lot,
Still gonna like him,
Always to be with!

Wanna wear his clothes,
Have to give commission,
Whenever he works for me,
Fight like a criminal,
Still I love my brother!

MONISHA

She was born in Villupuram but her native is Thirvannamalai (Erumpundi) Tamilnadu. She is 18. Her words are very pure and
the words are coming from her heart. She is kind one. She understood others feelings and also Control herself. She advices everyone who come to her and told their problem.
Twitter: Monisha.T

COMMON ONE

Dreaming is something that is common to all!
That is, Life is a dream…,
It doesn't belong to anyone and it is something common;
His dream is the most important thing to him!!
For someone who does not have a dream,
The dream is always a dream…
God decides everything...;
But how can determine when man has surpassed God?
So you have to live with a dream
That you should not be Dreamless……..!
Life is a though and rough path and
In that path one of the dreams plays a greater role….
So don't give up your dream for anyone……!!!

PRAGYA VERMA

Pragya Verma is born and raised in Prayagraj, Uttar Pradesh. She is currently pursuing Bachelor's in Computer Application. She is a poetess and a writer. She has done 60+ anthologies as a co-author and currently she's compiling her own anthology. You can follow her on Instagram: @wordsofpragya

Instagram handle: wordsofpragya

LET THEM DREAM

My dreams want me to fly,
Live freely like birds in the sky.
In all these chaos, I have listened to my heart,
It has made me move forward by using my art.

Strong competition, less opportunities,
Having dreams but full of insecurities.
In today's world, money is everything,
That's why; everyone is running after this thing.

This world has another definition of dream,
Mother-father wants their children to fulfil their dreams.
Nobody asked their child what they wanted to achieve,
That's why, they have stopped dreaming and started to compete.

Let them dream, let them decide,
Let them do what they want to do from inside.

PRATHAMESH PRAVIN NAIK

Basically he is student currently studying in standard 12th and write what he feels , he writes in yourquote app which is the most popular writing app and also shares his thoughts on Instagram. Thank you
*Instagram handle: rnqs_official_*

Living in dream is easy , but making it happen in our life is a real challenge. Often people dream big , but when it comes to make it happen in real life , they just lose hope. They just feel it's not thier cup of tea. But atleast if you try anything can happen. Just keep trying. You never know the very next minute you'll be successful. There are many examples of such sucess. So be ready..!! Gear up yourself. Work hard daily. Because "HE" is planning something unique for you but for that he needs your dedication towards it. Your daily hardwork towards it. Whenever you feel low HE'LL help you but if you lose hope he won't help you achieve your goal. It may take time , but SURELY gonna happen ONE DAY..!! HAVE PATIENCE..!!

PRAVEENA RAMESH

She is Praveena. she is currently pursuing her Bachelor's Degree in English literature. She is very much interesed in writing poem and quotes.
Instagram handle: Praveena893.

DREAM OF LIFE

- Think of your Dream move for it and achieve it.
- Our life began with dream and has no end for that.
- Start where you are; Use what you can and do what you can.
- Say goodbye to your past dream; and Say Hi to your new dreams.
- Don't get sad until your dreams gets successful.
- All our dreams will come true; if you have faith to pursue them.
- Don't dream your life; Live your life as dream.
- Don't step back of your dreams,oneday it will come true.

RASHMI BAWEJA

रश्मी इस कहानी की लेखिका बिल्कुल अपने नाम के अनुरूप ही सबके जीवन को प्रकाशित करती है।वे बहुत ही स्पष्टवादी है।वे फेसबुक पर HEART TOUCHING पेज
पर भी लिखती हैं।
https://www.facebook.com/rashmibaweja1993/अलग अलग विषयों पर वे बहुत अच्छा लिखती हैं। दूसरों के मनोभावों को वे बखूबी समझती हैं।
Instagram handle: rashmi_baweja13

सपने

हम चाहे तो हैताश होकर अपना सब कुछ हार जाए।
हम माने तो हर मुसीबत को हसते हुए पार कर जाएं।
ज़िन्दगी का सफर हमारे निर्णय पर ही निर्भर करता है।।
या तो हम अपने सपने पूरे करे या उन्हें अधूरा छोड़ दे।

काम छोटा हो या बड़ा मेहनत करने से क्यों डरा जाए।
लोग क्या कहेंगे इस बात को सोचकर आगे बढ़ने से क्यों रुक जाए।
लोगो का क्या है उनके कहने को अगर हम सोचते रहे तो।
या तो हम अपने सपने पूरे करे या उन्हें अधूरा छोड़ दे।

हारकर भी अगर जीत के सपनो को बरकरार रखा जाए।
जीत को हमेशा अपनी आंखों में सपनो की तरह संजोया जाए।
तो मुसीबते खुद हमे छोटी लगने लगेंगी पर तय हमे करना है।
या तो हम अपने सपने पूरे करे या उन्हें अधूरा छोड़ दे।

SAI GAYATHRI

She is Sai Gayathriwho pursues 2nd UG in Tamilnadu. Her passion is not at all writing but she started to write quotes for her relaxation. And those relaxation quotes automatically changed as her passion.
Instagram handle: iquotesbook

YOUR LIFE YOUR DREAM

"Yeah remember to dream big, don't think you can't able to achieve, dream big with hope because self confidence is very important. Always you need to carry your hope by your side. When you dream big you may face some negativity. Some may laugh at you, some may think your silly, even some will say you can't achieve. Please don't take their words into your ears. Show them your real side, by your success say them you can achieve anything it may be big or small by your results not by your words. Show your hidden talent for everyone"

SARASWETHA

She is Saraswetha. She is pursuing her B.A.English degree. She is from Villupuram, Tamil Nadu. She writes because of her love for English. She strongly believes in positive vibes. She is fond of writing Short stories and quotes in English.
Instagram handle: saras_swetha

SPRINKLING DREAMS

Dreams come true by hard work;
And not by luck or magic.

Life with a good dream gives,
Life with a beautiful future.

If you procrastinate your works,
you may lose your dreams.

Make your dream as a disease,
That doesn't have a medicine to cure it.

This world will identify you by your successful dream;
And not just by your name.

SHALINI

She is Shalini from villupuram. She is doing her graduation in bachelor of commerce her hobby is drawing. She has love on her sister which makes her to shower her words in the poem.

*Instagram handle: _freshfairy_*

SISTER

A sister is some,
Who loves from heart,
Shared our clothes,
Shared our shoes,
And everything,
Argument don't take place,
As our love tho,
Have many different views,
Also sacrifice for each other,
Finally,
We can't live without each,
Have same birthday date,
And blessed for that,
Everyone may be single born,
But we have born dually.

SHARMILA

Sharmila, currently doing undergraduate degree in nursing, staying in Pondicherry. She was an eventual writer loving to write short stories. Interested in writing moral stories inspired from personal experience of life. This story tells about a poor girl who struggles to achieve her dream.
Instagram handle: Sharmila6928sha

SURABHI'S DREAM

Here is a story about 25 years old girl. She was born in a small orthodox Brahmin joint family. She got admission in a Hindi medium school in her village. Her 10th STD result came she got a good mark and also got a place in a state merit list. On that occasion she had a press meeting and they asked her what was her dream on hearing this she became stunned at a moment because she never thought about this before and after a while she replied, "I want to become an IAS". Even though she was born in a poor family she worked hard day and night .She left her family and went to Delhi to purse her higher studies she struggled lot with no food, no rest and with lots of pain she cleared all the top prestigious exams and interview of India and she became a successful IAS.

SOFIYA MEHAKE

Sofiya Mehake was born at Mysore and brought up in Tindivanam. By this year she found her love for Hindi poetry.

Instagram handle: sprinkling_sparking_words

मेरी ख्वाबो की दुनिया

ख्वाबो की दुनिया थी बड़ी सुन्दर
थी बड़ी शांति मन के अंदर
वो दुनिया थी इस दुनिया से अलग
इस दुनिया में थे हम जुदा
वहां होगये हम एक दूजे के लिए सदा
लम्बी थी हमारी कहानी
नहीं बोलपावुंगी सिर्फ जुबानी
क्या था तेरा और मेरा रिश्ता?
करदु मैं अपनी जांनिसार
बोला था नहीं जी पावगे मेरे बिना
क्यूँ नहीं करते तुम अपने प्यार का इकरार?
हमेशा करुँगी तेरा इंतेज़ार
क्यूंकि इस दुनिया से परेह था हमारा प्यार
मेरी ख्वाबो की दुनिया
सिर्फ मेरी दुनिया

SWAYAMDEEPTA DAS

She is Swayamdeepta Das,residing in Hind motor,a suburban town in Hooghly district of West Bengal. She has passed class 12 from Vivekananda Academy and will pursue engineering. She loves music, sketching and is an ardent reader of crime fiction. She is a co-author of 61+ anthologies. She is a realistic person. She has also compiled and edited a book 'Pure Bliss' which is going to be published soon.

Instagram-swayamdeepta_das

Sapna toh tha uska gayika banne ka
Par kismat ko shayad kuchh aur hi manzoor tha
Maa baap use chikitsak bante dekhna chahte the
Unke sapne ko poora karne ke liye apni khwahish chhod di.

Daydreaming is a bad habit,
Stop thinking about the future
Live in the present
And enjoy it to your heart's content.

Dreams may come true but
Some people believe that dreams seen at dawn
Will definitely be fulfilled,
Change your mentality,stop believing in such superstitions.

VAISHALI

She isVaishali. Her parents are Lakshmanan and Padmavathi. She is studyingB.A.English 2nd year in Villupuram.

Instagram handle: Cuddle_by_happiness

DEAR ACHEIVERS

“Dream is the first step of achievement."
Dream will embossed like a nail. Dream makes a person as a complete different one. If our mind will change by seeing something, you just remember your past few insulted moments, it will never destroy.
"DREAM NEVER LET YOU SLEEP UNTILL YOU ACCOMPLISH YOUR TRIUMPH."
People without dream, please leave the world as soon as you can, because you guys are undesirable. We never wait for a big chance to achieve; we must do small things that will help us to rectify the mistakes.
"If you do the small things in a perfect manner, your dream chance will knock your door."

YAMINI SONA VAISHNAVI

Yamini Sona Vaishnavi is a budding writer. She lives in Madurai, Tamil Nadu. She pursues her III UG of graduation in English Literature. She loves to play with words and her passion is to write poems and short stories. She wishes to touch the hearts of readers through her poetry. She is already a co-author of 10 anthologies.

MY REAL FANTASY

I know I'm asleep, yet I feel your touch, hear you whisper and feel as if I'm dancing with you...
Oh! Mylove, why don't you let me doze and you yourself take a power nap for sometime...
Stop being awake and being kiddish!
Consider that you have been working the entire day and I've to wake up early...
We both need that short period to close our eyes together...
All of a sudden I hear you screaming “Darling! Stop talking to me in your dream!”...you hold me in your arms and wink...
It was a pleasant real fantasy my love...!

YASMIN

She has a Graceful and Sophisticated yet simple charm. She is an amiable. She is pursing graduation in the dept of Commerce (CA) from the University of Thiruvalluvar. She is 19 years old. She enlightened in TamilNadu. She is the one and only YASMIN.

A FANTASY DAY

How many Years?
How many Months & Days?
It acrossed while sleep and on imagination,
Thou it reminds to reach more.
It's the easiest thing to THINK,
But hardest to ATTAIN.
Hold it taut et nurture it, Think et Move on high.
Don't give up the happiness, which is
Buried many times inside.
Isn't just achieving the Goals?
Non it's indomitable.
A day pleased with gleam,
I know in due time, it will fall into places.
I draw out my own conclusions and complete the episode.
A day, it’s a day: It's a day of the DREAM DAY.

ZEEL MILISHIA

ZeelMilishiais from Ahmedabad, Gujarat. She is an excellent writer. Currently she is working as a CO author and a compiler. She loves to express her emotion and thoughts via poetry, shayari, stories. Till now she has been a part of 10 anthologies and had contributed to the process of compilation. *Instagram handle: @written_by_zeel / @zeel_milishia_13*

पहेली बारिश

ना जाने कहा है वोह मौसम हमारा,
जहा हम अपनी बाते किया करते थे।
आज भी याद है हमें हमारी पेहली बारिश,
दोनो भीगे थे एक साथ प्यार के रिश्ते मै ।

ANKITA PANDE

मेरा अब तक का सफ़र ये बात उसकी है जो बहुत महत्वकांशी है। उसकी अभिलाषा हमेशा से कुछ अलग करने की रही है। पर उस ने हमेशा कुछ और ही करने में अपना समय निकाल दिया। अब जीवन के तीस वर्ष निकल गए थे तब वह एक पत्नी, बहु,और एक माँ की जिम्मेदारी निभा रही थी। वो फिर से अपनी पहचान बनाने की कोशिश कर रही थी। शादी के पहले उसने इंजीनियरिंग की पढ़ाई पूरी कर के अच्छी कंपनी में नौकरी की थी। ग्रहणी होने के साथ साथ वो अपने जीवन में एक सकारात्मक परिवर्तन करना चाहती थी। अब उस ओर बढ़ रही है। वो अपने को ऊंचे मक़ाम पर देखना चाहती है।

Instagram handle: ankitajain8857

क़ुदरत को सम्भालो

कुदरत को संभाल
इसका रखो ख्याल
तुमने कर दी मुश्किल
अब धरती का दिल
तुमने तोड़ दिया
क़हर बरपा है,
ज़मीन ने उगली आग
आसमान से आई बिजली,
लहरें बनी सैलाब
संभल जा इंसान
बनकर हैवान
तूने किया सबको परेशान
इंसान बनकर
संवार ले गुलिस्तान

ANANDHI MURUGAN

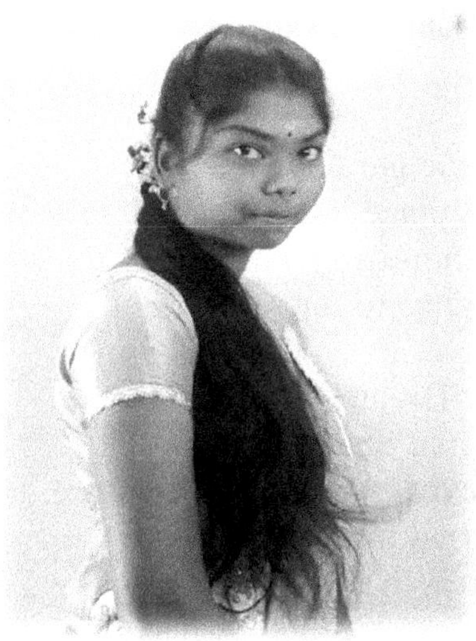

She is Anandhi from Villupuram; she studies B.A.Literature (Eng). She was interested to write poems. She dedicates this poem to all dreamers.

My dream my dream my dream
I want to fly like an eagle
Because its have sharply eyes
An eagle flies near the sky
Like that I want to fly with dreams

I want to become garden
It's a beautiful place like a heaven
All beings are admiring gardens
It's a real paradise to me

My Dream My Dream My Dream
I become just like Shakespeare
I want to achieve whatever in literature
I hope, and I trust myself,
My Dream surely will come true

SAICHARU

Herself Saicharu@CharulathaHails from Villupuram. In school days itself she loves to write. Her inspiration is based on her teacher Sugu Ma'am and Atchu, Madhumita (she is also a writer too). She started writing by poem and Quotes to her closed one. Her life makes colourful with her emotions and writing. This depicts is about a dream of Myself, her writing will make the readers not to impress by mind but impress by heart too...write hard and clear that makes u to comfort.

MIRACLES

The dream is different when compared with real way of its journey.
The mind that refuses to accept,
Because one day the dream will go away,
Or maybe achieved.

In search of the dawn of our lives.
We will realize the strength of the dream
Folding in the path of the dream,
We all are still kids who are longing.
Even that dream reaches every little space of your living,
We move towards the passage of excitement of the mind.
Let's begin to dream big,
There are so many dreams,
Let's insert one by one in our lives,
On the whole ,
Dream is the excitement of our life.

DEEBIKA

She is P. Deebika, a proud naturopath doing her final year in a well reputed institution at Chennai. Though she stuck her path towards science, her creativity and interest towards literature made her to write poems, quotes and essays as a leisure routine. Let us have a look how wisely she quoted her poem
Instagram handle: deebika_deeps

DREAM WITH LIFE EXISTENCE

Nature! What a cleverest craft you are!
Sketched out of pentagonal panel,
Tinted out of diverse chromatics,
Slumbered once beside your impressions,
Distracted out of notions with bhootas,
Dreamt once a planet without Fire,
But! How the universe be enlightened.
Dreamt once a planet without Earth,
But! How the universe be grounded.
Dreamt once a planet without Air,
But! How the universe be vitalised.
Dreamt once a planet without Water,
But! How the universe be energised.
Dreamt once a planet without Space,
But! How the universe be occupied.
Blended within fantasies of my vision,
Perceived existence on a lifeless planet,
Provoked out of panic visions from couch,
Realized the allegiance of renowned souls,
Admired the illustrious nature to be praised,
Dear, Rulers! Healers! Defenders! Destroyers!

"Pacify your dreams by aligning your lane along the path of perfection towards one's goal, to enlighten yourself as a predecessor than an achiever"

“Let your dreams be achieved by seeking a finely tuned balance between Ying and Yang"

"Carve your dreams and tint them with the shades of your kind towards the goal of your masterpiece to be sketched”

SANJOLI MITTAL

Sanjoli is a bibliomaniac and writer. She is currently pursuing MBA. She easily finds common interests with strangers and tends to make most people feel comfortable.
Instagram handle: sanjolimittal

IT MIGHT BE A DREAM

You went without
Saying a goodbye,
But you are still here,
You didn't die.
You are alive,
In every teardrop I shed.
I see your shadow, whenever I look ahead.
It might be a dream or a mirage,
The testament of my wilting hope, in life's corsage.
But these dreams are my only ray of light, when the sun goes down.
The straws I keep grasping at whenever I drown.

DIVYANK RAJ

इनका नाम दिव्यांक राज है। ये राज्य बिहार, जिला - पश्चिम चंपारण, शहर- बेतिया से है पेशे से एंड्रॉयड डेवलपर है एवम् लेखन में काफी रुचि रखते है 30+ एंथोल्जी में सह लेखक के रूप में रह चुके है इनकी एक ही सोच है अपने लेखनी से जीवन में परिवर्तन लाना एवम् सही दिशा देना समाज को। आप इन्हें इंस्टाग्राम आईडी @ divyankraj1 फेसबुक आईडी divyankraj तथा
ई मेल आईडी - divyankraj1@gmail.com
पर संपर्क कर सकते है
इनसे जुड़ सकते है।।

श्क़ विश्क

अपनी जुल्फो को तुम कुछ यूं सवार लो
लगा कर गले हमे बना गले का हार लो

की लगने लगे जन्नत ज़िन्दगी हसीन मुझे
कमी लगे बेशक खरीद पूरा बाज़ार लो

रातरानी हो तुम हो वो खूबसूरत चांद
भरकर बाहों में जरा लूट मेरा करार लो

कायनात भी मुरीद है हुस्न की तुम्हारे
कभी फुर्सत में इनको भी पुकार लो

चांद तारो की परवाह फिर नहीं होगी
संगमरमर की खुद को जो बना मीनार लो

रह भी नहीं सकता अब मै बिन तुम्हारे
एक दफा मुझे बना अपना शिकार लो

सांस भी अब तुम्हारा नाम लेकर चलती
हिफाजत करूंगा बना जो मुझे हथियार लो

KRISHNA MOTWANI

Krishna Motwani is a Student currently. She is a moody girl. She started writing in the month of June, 2020. She loves to write shayaris, small poems on love, family, friends, nature, and many more. She writes in her free time. She also writes some motivational quotes or poetries too and practices artworks also. She lives her life like a bird as bird flies freely and enjoys life like that she also lives her life freely and enjoy fullest.

*Instagram handle: @unique__blog_*

Girl loved a boy,
He was in front of her,
Boy came closer,
She was staring him, he asked why?

After a while boy went at her home
Both went for a walk alone,
They were talking with each other with happiness,
Boy asked to marry now, girl replied to have patience,
Boy was not having anyone known.

Two boys came from their back,
Boy died, because that another boy beaten him with knife,
She lost him before becoming his wife,
Now she has in her heart, a crack!

She scared,
Woked up and screamed,
And seen that was only an incident which she dreamed,
Went to her mother and hugged tight!

GOWRI

Gowri is the daughter of C.Bharathidasan and B.Rani. She is a third year literature student. She spends most of her time in writing .because, writing is the only thing,and she wants to do. This is the third anthology; she is working as a co-author. She wrote this poem with a hope of becoming a writer and a step towards her literary career.

MY LOST DREAM

My lost dream is you...
You're the one, who found the love in me
You're the first person in my life, to attain my love
You make me to smile, whenever I'm seeing you
You created the happiness in me with your actions
You allowed me to love you more with a small blink
You cherished me, without my Knowledge
But, after doing all these things...
Why did you leaved me?
You really don't know, how did I Suffered in that time
I waited almost three years for you
But, you didn't come...
Now, I accepted that you didn't accepted me
Thanks, for giving an enduring pain in my heart

SEHRISH FUZEL

Sehrish Fuzel is a graduate in B.COM Hons from Amity University Madhya Pradesh. She is currently pursuing her masters in Economics from IGNOU. She loves to read, write, sketch, watch TV series and listen to music. Besides this she is also very fond of travelling. She is currently working as a volunteer at the Bliss foundation and is also the social media Head at Scholars India network.
Instagram handle: sehrishfuzel

ALL WE HAVE IS NOW

Yesterday would never call us back,
The promise of tomorrow may not be fulfilled,
Yesterday is no longer with us,
Tomorrow seems like a mirage,
We are lost in cherishing the past,
And busy in pondering about what is yet to come.
We're recollecting our past,
And chasing tomorrow
And the present is all wasted...
We cannot bring the past back,
Worrying won't make our tomorrow better,
Why ruin the present then?
Let's live, love and laugh
Because all we have is now...

SACHIN BANOUDHIYA

Sachin Banoudhiya is an aspiring 21 year old Poet and author. He enjoys writing poetry, Doing Audio Poetries, quotes, articles and Loves to Edit Videos. He is a published poet and co-author. Most of his writings and accomplishments are displayed on the same. He aims to grow of vocabulary and develop for his readers; He is A Student of Bachelor of Science Currently a Hospital Staff, A Boy with So Many Responsibilities with Lot of Dreams...
Instagram handle: Sachin_banoudhiya

मेरे सपने पूरे हो गए क्या ?

कहानियों में उलझने का वक़्त था
टक टक करती घड़ी की सुई
मेरे मुकाम से नजदीकियां दिखा रही थी,
कायर सा रहने वाला इंसान
डर का मतलब भूल गया ??
ख़ुद के पैरों पर खड़ा होना
एक सपना हुआ करता था ,
जो मेरे पीठ पीछे बुराई करते थे ,
अब वही मुझे हौसला देने लग गए क्या ?
कल तक जो धुंधली सी दिखती देती थी,
आज पैरों तले दिखाई देती है ,
ये मेरी मंजिले है क्या ?
अच्छा तो मतलब मेरे सपने पूरे हो गए क्या ?

DIKSHA MOTWANI

Diksha is from Mumbai, Maharashtra. She use to pen down her feelings. She is an artist, singer, poet and writer as well.
Instagram handle: @radha_1229

YOU AND I

You and I,
Beyond this world, we will lie,
Love you most dear,
Losing you is my greatest fear.

Dream come true,
Only with you,
You are mine always,
With you, I am flawless.

A moon, yes you,
I have only you,
Stay with me dear,
I won't let you have a single tear.

Morning arrived,
For stopping you, I tried,
You left me alone,
After all, it was a dream of my only own.

JATA

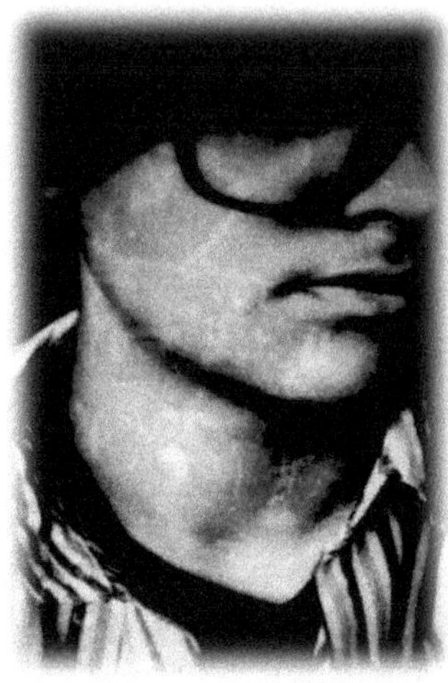

Jata_V, an instrument of Nature, existing in the Indian subcontinent. Time's person of the year 2006, Jata doesn't have a heart of its own. Alien to selfish Love and fellow human expressions. Currently Moon walking at the tributary where fantasy stream merges with roller coaster life.
Instagram handle: jata_v7

A STAR LIGHT'S JOURNEY TO YOUR EYES

Young and tender as fresh bloomed Tulips,
The journey to my dream began with a stirring smile
With a heart as glass and brain as a stone. Forced to taste the overripe fruits of life at such a young age
Made the eyes and mind too old to dance to the jazz...
Knew the goal in a fashion of perfect and pristine!
For a long time, searching for the path to start the journey
But they say that I'm already on-board.
Yet, in no way I can see the road distinctly... With this pace, this piece will either hit the peak or perish in the infinite ocean of misery...
Will this gloomy Epiphyllium ever see the Moonlight?
Will this melancholic sunflower ever see the Sunlight?

VIBHOR BIJOY

Vibhor Bijoy is a software engineer by profession and a poet by passion. He has been a part of various amazing anthologies. Besides writing he loves boxing, cooking, acting etc.

Instagram handle: dilsedoalfaaz

कहाँ गयी
कहाँ गयी वो रातें जिनसे मिलती थी सुकून भरी नींद
कहाँ गयी वो बातें जिनसे मिलती थी तस्सली के दो पल
और घटाते थे नफ़रत का बल
कहाँ गयी वो यादें जिनसे तालुक थे गहरे
और भावुक हो जाते सबके चेहरे
कहाँ गयी वो शोर भरे नारे
जिसे सुन थिरक उठते थे दिल के प्यारे मोर
कहाँ गयी वो दिलदार यारियाँ
जिनके साथ लगती थी प्यारी हर बदमाशियां
कहाँ गयी वो सड़कें
जहाँ मन कभी ना भटका
कहाँ गयी वो माफ़ी जिसे क्रोध की अग्नि ठंडी हो जाती थी काफी
कहाँ गयी वो रातें जिनसे मिलती थी सुकून भरी नींद
और मिलता था नया जूनून!!

KHUSHI GUPTA

Khushi is a writing enthusiast and a passionate and keen observer of literature with Creativity.....she is a graduation pursuing student who is on the long and soothing journey of exploring herself and the inner she. She has been the part of 15+ anthologies and currently working as Co author for four upcoming anthologies as well.

One night, I slept tight.
And saw some swirly dreams,
Dreams full of tears and screams.
Combining laughter and cheers,
Glory and victory from biggest fears.
Recording dreams and goals in mind,
Dreams which makes happy when rewind.
That beautiful feeling of one of a kind.
Dreams are the hopes full of emotions,
Which motivates us either in still or motion.
Dreaming was an ultimate pleasure,
Dreams are the one which leads to treasure.
Dreams are the driving force.
Revolves in mind while all the chores.

ELIA NAQVI

She is Elia. Having variant pet names few calls her Eli few calls Khushi and for few she is chini (sugar). She is trying to make her obsession as her profession. By god grace and parents are her forever mates

Instagram handle: anonymous.extrovert&naqvi.elia

Batao me kya karu
Mere sapno ko mai baya kaise karu?
Kya batau or kya me likhu!
Bachpan se khudko khush karu
Bade hoke maa ba ap kadil bharu
Khel me sab se aage me rahu,
Padhte waqt likhai ke spne bunu
Dil se me mehnat karu,
Par kuch bat tassali na paasaku,
Per himmat na haar mai phir aage badhu,
Sab se saamne khudko prove karu,
Parindo se ucha mai ud saku,
Apne maa baap ko har khushi de saku,
Duniya me Khubsurat na hoke khubsurti banu,
Har muflis ki madad sab se pehle mai karu,
Haste haste kai bar ro padu,
Or khud hi apne assu pochlu,
Apne sapno ko mai pura karu,
Kya batau kya mai karu,
Naam chupakar kya mai karu,
Khudko "ELIA" bata apne arman pure karu,

ANINDITA BHATTACHARYA

Anindita Bhattacharya is a sixteen year old young lady who hails from the pittsburgh of India- Jamshedpur, studying in a well known institution- N.H.E.S.A flawless flawed , perfectly imperfect soul who has worked in many National as well as in International anthologies as a co author. A bibliophile, selenophile, pluviophile, logophile, ceraunophile and a logastellus too. She is also an orator and never feels shy in speaking her beliefs, giving her whole heart to it. *Instagram handle*
*@moonlit..feathers_@readers..point_*

Driving away the vast ocean of clouds,
Peers the bewitching selene,
Mystique as always, in the starry crowd.

Moonlight spilled on the green grass,
Bestowed with enthral, as if,
Waiting for the darkness to pass.

Soaked in the godly silver,
Are the enchanting petals,
Before my eyes that always will linger.

Drenched is the lake in divinity,
Full of beauty and magic,
Making me dream to establish my little infinity.

PRATHAM MITTAL

He is very positive, kind, helpful, friendly and happy soul. His passion is painting and writing. He has won many competitions, published in many books, participated in international writing competitions.

Instagram handle: @_pratham2426

“Life is full of beauty. Notice it. Notice the bumble bee, the small child, and the smiling faces. Smell the rain, and feel the wind. Live your life to the fullest potential, and fight for your dreams.”

BICKEY MANDAL

He is Bickey Mandal from Jharkhand. With his poetries he is trying to connect myself with others. He is passionate about my works because he loves what he does. He has a steady source of motivations that drives him to do my best. You can contact him through
Instagram handle: bickey_ki_ankahi_baatein

सपने जो कभी कभी ही पूरे होते है

क्यू हर पल में तुम्हें याद करता हूं ।
क्यू हर पल में तेरी ख्वाहिशें रखता हूं ।

ख्वाहिशें तो सबके होते है,
पर पूरे कुछ ही के होते है।

क्या ये मेरी आदत हो गई ।
या बन गई मेरी कोई मजबूरी ।
जो हर वक़्त तेरा ही सपना देखता हू।

क्यू में हर पल सिर्फ तुम्हे चाहता हूं ।
क्यू में अपने आप को खोना चाहता हूं ।
में सिर्फ और सिर्फ तुम्हारा होना चाहता हूं ।

नींद तो पूरे होते नहीं मेरे,
और चला में अपने सपने पूरे करने,
भूल के सारे अपने दुखरे ।

SANIYA MAHEK

She is Saniya Mahek from Hyderabad, studying degree. She is an ardent writer and love to explore about human behaviour (psychology). She is seeking a freelance job. Sheloves to read books.

Instagram handle: syedaosmium

DREAMS

Full of emotions and oceans of love
Where there's no fake owe
In an blink of an eye
Sky is covered with a blanket of stars and moon

Glittering stars with twinkling nights
Of comforts and delight.
Sleepy, woozy soul striving to hit the sack, but mind is compact.

Dozed off with pleasant thoughts
And a Butterfly with colourful wings,
A bird sing's and Ding's with a soothing voice.
Far away from the world conspiracies and plots

Humongous fall of milk
Treasure of tea leaves with an attractive fragrance
Besides, a huge tree dressed in silk.
Where there's a lot of treasure, I can conquer without any pressure
An abundance of leisure,wanna seize the time to look after my heart

PRIYA DAS

Priya Das is a teenager with optimistic look to worldly life. She is born and brought up in Jamshedpur. She is co author of several other books and loves to provide shape to her thoughts. You can contact her through email her at pdas72108@gmail.com

Instagram handle- @inexorable_voice

Dear success
I wish I could connect with you
Not through just pocms but by a bond
Though it's not possible I knew
I adore you or say carry your fond
People say it's possible to achieve you
But I know I am not alone, there are many in the queue
Still I decided to fight for getting you
Will find you soon dear success, hope you have a clue

NIKHIL JAIN

He's Nikhil Jain from Dhule, Maharashtra. He's 25 years old. He joined the family business and handled supermarket and utensils shop for 1 year and started wholesaling of Cp fittings and sanitary ware. He likes to share his knowledge with others and he's a marketing and sales trainee. He loves to write because it's the best way to express your feelings and his hobby is Jugaad. He has been a part of 19 anthologies so far and many more in the process of compilation. He uses a simple language in his Shayari and poetry, which could be easily understood and which relates to every human. *Instagram handle: love.vibes143*

अंबर तले धरा पर बैठे बैठे,
एक गहरी सोच में सो गया,
जाने कब ये दिन ढल गया,
ना मौसम ना वक़्त का पता चला,
मैं अपने सपनों की दुनिया में खो गया।

हर तरफ जहा खुशियों की बहार थी,
दिन हसीन और रातें गुलज़ार थी,
परेशानियों, दुखों का तनिक भी अंश ना था
ऐसे कल्पनाओं के संसार में मैं पहुंच गया,
मैं अपने ही सपनों की दुनिया में खो गया।

आंखों में जहा लाज और शर्म का बसेरा था,
बड़ों के लिए नज़रों में आदर सम्मान पसरा था,
छोटों के लिए दिलों में मोहब्ब्त काम ना थी,
प्यार और अपनेपन की वो एक अनोखी दुनिया थी,
एक पल के लिए तो मैं उसी दुनिया का हो गया,
मैं अपने ही सपनों की दुनिया में खो गया।।

LEENA DEVI NEDUNCHEZHIYAN

She is Leena Devi She is currently pursuing her Bachelor's Degree in English Literature She is very interested on writing quotes, short stories, prose. She is also interested in playing volley ball as well basket ball

Instagram handle: Lonely_heart_leens

SCARY DREAM

Dreams are the most beautiful ones,
It gives us want we want even if it's for a moment,
It makes us think more,
Just like that, a day I had a dream,
I was scared because I was in an orphanage,
I was kidnapped from the orphanage,
I was all alone,
It made me to realize the pain of an orphan,
I was afraid to be alone for the first time,
It made to feel the pain of not having someone,
It made me to cherish the life I live with my family,
And it also gave me tons of hope to develop myself,
Because I want to make someone's life better,
This dream wasn't a nightmare,
It was an inspiration to me,
To help the people in need,
I will stick on to my hope,
One day I'll build a safe home to the orphans

Flairs and Glairs, a platform by a student for the students. We are esteemed youth struggling to carve out our path for our future and we follow a basic mindset Since everyone is not born with all-round skills. Joining hands with people who are born to execute it with perfection is the best way to evolve. Self-Evolution is the need of the hour but, evolving as a community is what we strive for. The initiative as kickstarted by, Founder- Mr. Shubham Shah with the motive to utilize the skillset and talent of writing has now a team of 10+ people who are actively participating into newer forms of learning and discovering talents among youngsters. We Provide platform and services like Publishing opportunities, Open mics, Workshops, Hands-on training. Operating with Brand Name of Flairs and Glairs (Publication House), we offer the chance of elevating a passionate writer to an esteemed author With Brand name Teekhe Zasbaaat. We bring to you an opportunity to get accustomed with the Public Speaking and Presenting of Thoughts along with regular challenges to brush up your inking spirit. The newest initiative to extend our services we introduced in a new writing Platform- The Glittering Fables and Ink Over Tears.

We Choose to Fly Like A Falcon than to be

a Leg Pulling Crab.

To Know More: Infoline – 7781900870
Mail Us At-
flairsandglairs@gmail.com / info@flairsandglairs.in
Or Visit is at
www.flairsandglairs.com / www.flairsandglairs.in
Social Handles- @flairsandglairs @teekhezasbaaat

www.ingramcontent.com/pod-product-compliance
Ingram Content Group UK Ltd.
Pitfield, Milton Keynes, MK11 3LW, UK
UKHW022005190726
13853UKWH00004B/1749